SLAPSHOT

Emerald City Thunder

C.M. KANE

COPYRIGHT

Editing & book design by Maggie Kern @ Ms.K Edits

Cover art by Golden Czermak @ Furios Fotog

DEDICATION

For those who overcome the most terrible things, and those who get them to the win.

PROLOGUE

K aia...

"Welcome to Panacea."

Mr. Wilsor.... No, he said to call him Remi, had called himself "Mr. Fun" and was tasked with taking me around the office and walking me through all the paperwork. I'll admit, I was initially intimidated, but he set me at ease pretty quickly.

"Your resume is amazing, and we're thrilled to have you here," he said.

"I appreciate that," I said.

My resume, as he called it, consisted of my college course load, including the tutoring I did at the University, my internship after I graduated, and a whole lot of volunteer stuff that didn't line my pockets in any way, shape, or form. I'd found a way to pay for college and get through that time, but it hadn't been the best decision. Sometimes you choose a path without looking at how it might come back and bite you in the ass. Coming to Seattle and changing my name had been the right choice. It didn't erase my past, but hopefully, it would keep it from finding me.

"You should fit in nicely," he continued. "This is a pretty

great place to work. Good pay, decent benefits, and the perks that come up randomly are also amazing."

"That's what I've found from my research," I said. "You're community-minded, teaming up with some awesome charitable foundations, and just going out and doing good in the community. It's something I've always strived for and the kind of footprint and legacy I want to leave behind."

"Let's get you set up with a station so you can work on that legacy," he said.

The rest of the first day was as boring as any other, but it was nice to finally be using the degree I worked so hard to obtain. One of the things I'd noticed about the company, and honestly the biggest draw, was that they were very balanced in their diversity. Between the women who held positions of power, to people of color who ran entire divisions, to the clear balance of belief groups and lifestyles, they were one of the few big companies that felt like you could be whoever you wanted to be and still fit in.

While my parents were good at giving me a leg up, their drama was something I was glad to put behind me. It was another reason I chose Panacea and only looked at companies on the West Coast. Seattle was a better fit all around. It had everything I wanted with a decent cost of living, so long as you got out of the general downtown area. I did, however, notice that the Seattle Freeze, as it was coined, existed on the streets. Inside the company, people were warm, but walk down the streets, or step into the Pike Place Market, and aside from saying "excuse me," you were an island among others.

After the first week, I felt like I was settled and had even made a couple of friends within my section of the company. Drinks out on Friday night were fun, and letting loose a little, even while staying in control, was exactly what I needed after my first full week on the job.

CHAPTER ONE

FOUR YEARS LATER...

L ogan...

"Are you serious?" I asked my agent.

Michael Porter had been a godsend when I first met him. He'd walked me through the draft process, helped me with my contract, and explained everything in terms my stupid brain could understand. He kept me level headed the first couple of years, talked to me about my reputation, and how he was hearing from the team that they were shopping me around. I'd asked him to tell me how to fix the situation, and he'd come back with the trade.

"Look," he said. "This is a chance for you to make a change. Get out of Detroit and find a clean slate."

"But they're an expansion team," I complained.

"Logan," he said. "You either go to Seattle, or you end up in some farm system, wasting away until your legs are shot and you can't skate anymore."

He was right. I'd done enough shit that I'd sort of become the league's black sheep. I was on the bench more than on the ice, which didn't sit well with me. Sure, they threw me out there when they wanted muscle, but otherwise, I had a bad reputation. It wasn't unfounded, though. Everything I had was left on the ice, and I didn't hold back at all. I'd fought for the college scholarship, fought to get drafted early, and worked my ass off to get to the top. Now, I was being shipped off to damn near Siberia to a brand new team that was far away from everything I'd known.

"Please tell me they at least are offering a decent salary," I said, realizing I had done this to myself.

"So long as you behave," he replied. "It's comparable to what you're getting now, but with some added incentives. They're taking a chance on you, Logan. Something most of the other teams passed on. This is your chance for a fresh start, but you're gonna have to work for it."

"Fuck," I muttered. "I guess it's my own fault."

"You're not wrong," he said. "Seattle's conditions are strict, and you're gonna have to be on your best behavior. Your extracurricular activities need to stop."

I nodded, noting the piercing look he was giving me.

"Logan," he said, and I raised my eyes to him. "You're only twenty-five. You have a whole life ahead of you. Don't throw everything away on a flight of fancy. Buckle down, do your job, play the game, and get over the hump. Head down, skates on ice, and stick doing what it's supposed to. Keep your dick in your pants and stay out of trouble."

"Yes, Dad," I said.

"I'm not your parent," he said. "If I was, I'd've beat your ass for your actions right off the bat. I warned you back when we first met that I would do whatever I could to make sure you got everything we both knew you deserved. You haven't held up your end of the bargain, and we both know it. This is the last chance I'm gonna give you. You fuck this up, I'm gone. I have too many other kids who want to do this and who are making the sacrifices you should have. They deserve to get more of my attention than someone who's taken up more time than he deserved."

"I know," I said. "For what it's worth, I hear you. I don't want to give up on my dream, and I don't want you to give up on me, either."

"Then prove it," he said. "Get your ass on a plane and get to Seattle. I'll arrange for your stuff to be shipped out once you've found a place. For now, you're set up in a team apartment. Remember, the entire league is watching."

I stood up from the cush chair I'd been sitting in as he did. He shook my hand, and I turned and walked out of the office and to the elevator. Climbing into my car, I headed to my condo to pack a bag and head to the next step in my career. It wasn't where I wanted to go, but I only had myself to blame.

CHAPTER TWO

K aia...

"Aren't you at least a little excited about the event?" Carmen asked as we walked into the bar for this month's happy hour get-together.

We'd become fast friends when I first started, and the more time we spent together, the more she felt like the sister I never had. For the first time in my life, I felt like I was my own person instead of someone's daughter, and that was a pretty great thing. I loved my parents, but their bitter divorce gave me a whole lot of trauma that therapy could only do so much to alleviate. Still, I was actually fairly levelheaded.

"Almost every athlete I've ever met has been soft between the ears and hard in all the wrong places," I replied.

"Don't say that too loud around Kylie," she replied.

"Oh, I won't," I replied.

Kylie was our supervisor, and she was married to a player from the baseball team in Seattle. He was the first jock I met who didn't seem like just a hunk of meat packaged nicely.

"Cole seems like he's actually got a brain," I added.

Sure, my experience with jocks was making sure they passed their classes in college so the school could use them on the field, but most of them just wanted me to do their work, then let them do me as payment. Fortunately, the school paid me, so I didn't have to deal with that much. A few of the girls who tutored them found out the hard way that pretty looks don't always contain a pretty inside. Thankfully, the school pushed hard to ensure that those of us who did the tutoring were safe.

The bar was pretty packed, which was to be expected on a Friday night. Our group had commandeered a back set of tables, giving us plenty of space to spread out and still be close together.

"There they are," Nadia said. "We thought you guys got lost on the way over."

"It's practically across the street," Carmen replied. "We just had to finish things up."

"Kylie cracking the whip?" she asked.

"Not at all," I said as I slid onto a tall barstool. "Not all of us are freakishly fast with projects like you."

Nadia rolled her eyes at me, and I stuck my tongue out at her. We both laughed like we were twelve. Carmen just shook her head because she knew how we were.

"I'm going to get a drink," she said. "I'll bring you two back a couple of Shirley Temples, since adding alcohol seems like a bad idea."

"Here," I said, handing her a couple of twenties. "Get my usual for me?"

She took the money and headed to the bar.

"I am so freaking excited for next weekend," Nadia said. "Hockey boys are fucking hot."

"And usually dumb," I replied.

"I don't think so," she said. "I've watched some of the interviews with the players the team is getting, and they actually sound like they know some things."

"Knowing how to skate and hit people doesn't make them smart," I said, spinning the coaster that was on the table. "In fact, if they were smart, they'd stay off the ice. Most of them get serious brain damage and lose teeth from all the hits they take."

"Yeah," she agreed. "The lost teeth thing kinda makes them a little weird looking. But they're rich, so they could just replace the teeth. Why don't they do that?"

"Because losing a tooth is one thing," I explained, having asked this question while tutoring. "Knocking out an implant is worse and way more expensive. Most of them just have fake teeth they wear when they aren't on the ice."

"How do you know so much?" she asked.

"What does she know?" Carmen asked as she came back with our drinks.

"Hockey," Nadia said. "We were talking about next weekend."

"Oh, yeah," Carmen said. "She said she wasn't excited."

"I heard," Nadia replied. "Guess we're just gonna have to drag her with us, shove her up against some sexy guy, and see what happens."

"What's gonna happen," I said. "Is that guy gonna be pissed cause I'm gonna shove him over and away from me, then turn on you and smack you upside the head."

"Okay, okay," Nadia said, holding her hands up in front of herself. "Calm down, girl."

"Maybe one of them will make you change your mind," Carmen said.

"I sincerely doubt it," I said. "I've dealt with enough of them to last me a lifetime. When I say I know how they are, trust me."

"Hold up," Nadia said, leaning in. "You dated a hockey player?"

"Sure haven't," I said. "But I tutored several, and they all wanted to pay me with 'favors' instead of money."

"And you didn't go for it?"

"Not a chance," I said. "I saw how the other girls they

used ended up feeling like absolute shit. I already felt that way, so there was no need to pile more on. Besides, most of them could barely hold a conversation, and I want to be respected in every relationship. None of them fit the bill."

"Girl, you got secrets," Carmen said. "We are definitely gonna have to check out the players you tutored 'cause I need to see what fine men you passed on. Do you still have their numbers?"

"Yeah, no," I said, taking a sip of my drink.

"Then what good are you?" Nadia asked.

I pinned her with a stare, stuck my tongue out, and we all broke up laughing again. I loved my job, the team I worked with, and felt like Seattle was gonna be home to me.

CHAPTER THREE

L ogan...

"Tonight is all about optics," Brian Lawrence, one of the team's owners, said. "Panacea is a company that holds power here in the greater Puget Sound area, and hosting them tonight will be the first step in coming together. I know you guys don't like the glad-handing, but they hold a few purse strings. It isn't too much to ask that you play nice with the folks who sign your checks."

Between moving to a totally different state, trying to get adjusted to the city, and figuring out how to even function with all the cloud cover, I had been struggling, to say the least. This whole team event thing the owners were doing was bullshit as far as I was concerned, but he did make a good point. Biting the hand that feeds you wasn't the way to go. I'd bitten enough hands that I was down to taking whatever scraps I could find.

My manager told me to play nice, do whatever was asked of me, and go above and beyond to ingratiate myself to the new team. They weren't hockey people. They were businessmen, and they would treat the team like a business. That meant that if someone wasn't pulling their weight or were being too big of dicks, they wouldn't hesitate to cut them out. With my attitude, I'd become the one who would be the first to go. It chapped my hide to think they'd cut me, but I knew it was true.

We'd all cleaned ourselves up, dressed in our finest, and were in the locker room just waiting for all the big wigs to get there. Once that happened, we'd be introduced as the newest franchise in the National Hockey League. They'd already talked about pushing for the playoffs, and we hadn't had but a handful of practices yet. Still, it was nice that I wasn't the only fuckup on the team.

"We gonna be allowed to fuck any hot chicks that come?" Shields asked under his breath.

I damn near choked, trying to hold the laugh in.

"Something you want to share?" the owner asked.

"No, sir," I said. "Just caught a bit of water in the wrong pipe."

I held up the water bottle I had as a show, but I was pretty sure he hadn't bought it.

"As I was saying," he continued, droning on in the monotone voice most businessmen had, nearly lulling me to sleep.

Finally, after an excruciating eternity, he ended his long-winded monologue, handed the floor to the coach, and turned to leave the locker room.

"One more thing," he said, turning back to us. "I know how much you guys like to… keep company, so to speak. But please don't do that with *this* company. Keep it professional, gents."

This time, I did chuckle, along with several of the other players. Coach was a lot less politically correct once the man with the checkbook left.

"Like he said," Coach barked, and we all waited. "Keep your sticks in your pants."

NEARLY AN HOUR INTO THE EVENT, my feet were screaming. I'd forgotten to pack my good dress shoes and had to grab something on the way in. Sitting at one of the tables along the side of the big event space, I watched as several women prowled the crowd, looking for someone to take care of them. And the brass tried to make us keep things kosher.

"Can I sit here?" a blonde woman asked.

"Sure," I said with a shrug.

"I don't know why I thought heels were a good idea," she mumbled, pulling one of her shoes off and massaging her foot. "Sorry," she said when she looked over at me.

"Completely fine," I replied. "I'm dealing with the same issue."

"You're wearing heels?" she asked, looking like I'd said something funny.

"Just the wrong shoes," I replied. "My good ones are still in Detroit."

"Ooh, that sucks," she said.

"Yeah," I replied.

"You good if I take them off and prop them on the chair?" she asked.

"Kinda wanna do the same thing," I replied. "Here," I said, turning toward her. "Gimme your foot."

She looked at me like I'd sprouted another head but did as I asked, turning and raising her foot onto the chair between us. I reached out but paused, looking at her to give me the go-ahead. With a nod, I slid my hand along her foot, pressing my thumb into the arch, and the sigh I got was exactly what I expected. Kneading her foot, sliding from heel to toe, she relaxed even more until she finally let out another long sigh.

"Gimme the other one," I said.

She did, sliding it along her leg until it was next to the one

I'd just been manhandling. Again, she relaxed once I'd gotten going, her head sort of tipping back and closing her eyes.

"Hey," I heard, and her eyes snapped up. "I thought you said they were all meatheads."

Pulling on her feet, she tried to get free, but I held her fast.

"Carmen," she said, then turned to glare at me.

"Let her go," Carmen said, her hands on her hips.

"You're interrupting," I replied, my voice low.

I felt her shudder but bit the smile that threatened to show.

"Pretty sure she's not interested," Carmen said.

"Please," the woman said, her eyes begging me.

"I don't think so," I replied, not letting her out of my grip.

"I'll go get security," Carmen said.

"No," the woman said, a sharp bark almost. "It's fine, Carmen. I'm fine."

Carmen locked at me like she was memorizing my face, looked back at my mystery woman, and then back at me.

"I'm watching you," she said, then turned on her heels and stomped away.

Letting out a sigh, the woman turned to me again.

"I swear," she said, almost to herself. "Guys are all Neanderthals."

CHAPTER FOUR

Kaia...

As much as I tried, I couldn't shake the feeling that Carmen was gonna spread some shit around, and it was all gonna fall back on me.

"Damnit," I grumbled.

"Hey," the guy said, still holding my foot hostage. I looked at him and he had a question in his eyes that I couldn't interpret, so I waited him out. "She gonna be a problem?" he asked, finally.

"Who knows?" I said with a shrug.

"I didn't mean to cause an issue," he said, his voice just loud enough for me to hear.

"It's not your fault," I replied. "It's these fucking shoes."

"Still," he said, pressing a thumb into my arch so hard I nearly saw stars before he slowly released the pressure.

"Whatever it is you do for a living," I said. "You need to add masseuse to your resume. I figured I'd be down for the entire weekend after this thing."

"Happy to oblige," he said. "I'm Logan."

"Nice to officially meet you," I replied. "I'm Kaia."

"Why does that name sound familiar?" he asked, but

whether it was me he was asking, I didn't know. "Wait," he said after the wheels in his head started to crank. "Did you go to the University of Minnesota?"

My eyes widened because there was no way he could have known that unless I'd tutored him. Racking my brain, I went through every name I could think of for players who had crossed my path, but Logan didn't come up.

"How did you know?" I asked him.

"Well, ain't that just the shit?" he said, his smile growing. "I think you tutored me in one of my classes. Don't know which one, though, cause I needed help in damn near everything."

I tried to pull my foot out of his grasp again, but he had a death grip on it. He was looking at me now. Really looking, and I felt entirely too vulnerable. He was a big guy, most players were, and he had ahold of my feet, which put me at an extreme disadvantage. Something must have crossed my face because, all of a sudden, he let my feet go. I quickly pulled them back, slicing into the cursed heels that were on the floor. If I was gonna get away from him, I needed to have my shoes on.

"Sorry," he said and actually looked like he meant it. "It just threw me for a loop. I haven't thought about college in years. Never in a million years did I think I'd run into someone who wasn't connected to hockey."

"It's one of the reasons I moved out here," I said, although why I was explaining myself to him, I didn't know.

"I take it you work for the company," he said.

It wasn't a question, but I felt like I had to answer it, anyway. "I do," I said. "For a few years, now."

"You doing okay?" Remi asked, and I startled and looked at him.

"I'm fine," I said, and could see Carmen behind him, along with Nadia. "Carmen, I said I was fine."

"Well," she said. "You didn't look fine, and he was holding your feet."

"Oh my God," I said, glaring. "My feet are killing me because *someone* insisted that I wear heels. So, if it's anyone's fault, it's yours."

She had the grace to look embarrassed, at least, so I scored one there.

"I'm Logan Knox," he said as he stood up and held his hand out to Remi.

"Nice to meet you," Remi said, taking his hand.

Remi was tall, but Logan was, too. The thing Logan had that Remi didn't was the muscle mass. His shoulders were broad, and his thighs were like tree trunks. Much as I hated athletes for their lack of brains, they were nice to look at. College me would be chastising myself for even thinking about this man in any other way than a brute, but mid-twenties me was definitely appreciating the physicality of the man next to me.

"...so I just wanted to check on her," Remi said. I looked up to see Carmen smirking behind his back.

"I'm fine," I said. "Just needed to give my feet a break, and Logan was kind enough to assist in working out the tight muscles."

"Comes with my job," Logan said. "Our feet are the foundation of our profession, so keeping them in shape is important."

"Well," Remi said, looking at me. "If you're good..."

He trailed off, clearly giving me an out if I wanted it.

"I am," I said, smiling.

"Great," he replied. "Carmen, Nadia, let's find Kylie and see what she's doing."

"I was thinking—"

"Now," he said, clearly taking them away so I had my privacy back. "She's got it handled."

Once they were gone, I let out a breath and then looked at Logan.

CHAPTER FIVE

L ogan...

"Your friends seemed surprised," I said.

"I've made it no secret about how I feel about athletes," she replied. "You surprise me, though."

"How's that?" I asked as I sat back down, this time in the chair right next to her. If it made her uncomfortable, she didn't let on.

"You're right that I likely tutored you," she said. "And most, if not all, of the athletes I worked with, were dumber than a box of rocks. No offense."

"None taken," I said. "I was an idiot when I was in school. Truth be told, I've been an idiot most of my life."

"You figured out how to make playing a game work for you," she said. "I have to go into an office every day and do someone else's work, only to get a small portion of what is garnered by the work I do."

"You sound bitter," I said.

"I'm not," she said. "Not really. I mean, given the option, I'd love to be financially independent enough to not have to do an actual job. But I'm kinda stuck until I win the lottery or someone rich dies and leaves everything to me."

"You could always marry a rich guy," I said. "Someone to take care of you, pay your bills, buy you fancy cars. You know."

"I'm not interested in finding a sugar daddy," she said. "If I'm gonna be with someone, they better be in it for the right reasons. Conversation and humor are high on my needs list. My guess is that I'll end up settling, though. I mean, my mom keeps bugging me for grandkids, but I know how my parents were, and I don't wanna give that kind of trauma to a kid."

"If you found someone who fit your criteria, what would you do?" I asked.

"You proposing?" she asked back.

"Just figuring out what makes you tick," I said. "You're sexy, and I like sexy. But I'm a dumb jock, so I'll probably fail you at everything you want."

"Maybe not everything," she said, a slight smile curving her lips.

"Oh yeah?"

"You do hold certain attributes that I have on my list," she said, her smile growing.

"I do, do I?" I teased.

She shifted in her seat. I wasn't sure if it was because she was uncomfortable, or she wanted to get closer to me. I was feeling a bit uncomfortable myself, but I'd be damned if I'd show it. Never give the competition an edge. If they know your weakness, they'll exploit it.

"To be honest, I never much cared for a meathead," she said. "All brawn and no brain. Damn near every guy I tutored tried to get me to take their payment in trade, if you know what I mean, instead of the money the school was paying me. It wasn't even like they were losing out on the money. I think they all just wanted to see how many nerdy girl's panties they could get into."

"Most of us did," I said, surprising myself.

"I'm shocked," she said, her face a sarcastic mask of

surprise. "You, this kind and caring man who massaged my feet, was just looking to get some?"

"Not tonight," I said. "We've been warned to keep our sticks in our pants."

"I suppose you always do what you're told, too."

Oh, now she was teasing for real. I slid my arm around the back of her chair, shifting myself to lean more toward her. My other hand went to her knee, which was covered in a stocking. I hadn't noticed how short her dress was when she sat down and thought it was below her knee when she put her feet up. She either pulled it up, or it was shorter than I thought.

"I rarely do what I'm told," I said, my voice low, my hand squeezing her knee. "Unless it's something I wanted to do anyway."

"And if I told you your hand was too far away from where it should be?"

Her raised eyebrow was like a challenge to me, but I had to be careful. We were in a crowded convention center with eyes all around us, many of which could fuck us over, and not in the way I wanted to fuck her. Glancing up, I saw people were milling around, but no one was really looking our way. When I turned back to her, she looked like the cat that ate the canary.

"What?" I asked.

"You worried about getting in trouble?"

"Yeah," I said. "I've gotta be careful. My leash is short, and one step off the path could end my career."

Her hand gripped my wrist, her knees separated a bit, and she slid my hand up her thigh, just *this* close to the Promised Land I wanted to get to. Fuck me if she wasn't wearing stockings and a garter belt. With her other hand, she flipped her skirt over my hand, hiding what I was doing or what I was gonna be doing in just a hot minute.

"How far you gonna let me go?" I asked, my voice low enough that she was the only one who could hear me.

"Try me," she said.

"Oh, no," I replied. "I know how that play ends. You're gonna have to be explicit in what you want me to do. I won't go any farther than you tell me to, and if you say stop, it stops."

CHAPTER SIX

K aia...
He was so close I could smell the aftershave or whatever he'd put on, and it was definitely making me stupid. This was such a bad idea, but I couldn't stop myself. He was fucking hot in so many ways and not nearly as stupid as the guys in college were. Either that, or he'd perfected the act of sounding smart when he had to. If I asked him to do some sort of algebra problem, he'd probably lose his mind.

"I don't suppose you know of anywhere we might be alone, do you?" I asked because, yeah, I was gonna go that far.

"New stadium," he said. "This is the first time I've been inside. I just got to town a week ago, and everything I'd done with the club has been at the practice facility."

"Shit," I said.

"I suppose I could take you on a tour of the locker room," he said.

"Maybe the visitors' locker room?" I asked. "You know, in case there are trade secrets in an office somewhere or something."

"I like the way you think," he said, squeezing my thigh, but still a hair's breadth away from where I really wanted him. "Do you think they'd notice us if we just sort of walked out?"

I looked up and out at the crowd in the space, wondering where my friends had gotten off to or if I even wanted to know. If they saw me leave with him, they'd shit bricks. Fuck, I'd probably be the talk of office gossip for months. Still, I really wanted him. It had been entirely too long since I'd gotten anything other than my battery-operated boyfriend, and that was getting old.

When I looked back at him, he hadn't moved. His eyes were bright, but not like he was drunk. No, he had a hunger in them that sparked my own desire and the need to get somewhere a little less crowded.

"Come on," I said, standing up.

He stood with me, his hand leaving my thigh but taking up residence at the small of my back. The heat radiating from him was like a furnace, and I wanted to let him heat up every damn part of my body.

"This way," he said, steering me with his hand toward the edge of the room. "Anyone asks, we're on a tour to go see the ice."

His breath rushed across my ear, hot and close, and I damn near lost my footing from it. He gripped my elbow, steadying me, and propelled me toward a door I hadn't noticed until just now. Stepping through, the sound slowly disappeared as it closed behind us. The hallway was industrial, like it was meant for staff, not guests, and I assumed it was. Likely where any number of the support people for the team would be traveling to and from one point to the next.

Without any covering on the floor, our footsteps were louder than I'd like, and it was mostly my fucking heels. I didn't want to get caught, but I wasn't sure I wanted to pull them off, either.

"Hang on," I said, stopping. I listened, trying to see if I could hear anyone coming. Thankfully, it was all quiet, and I let out a little sigh of relief. "Okay," I said, turning to him. "What?"

"You are fucking gorgeous," he said, his voice a low timber I felt more than heard.

His hand slid along my cheek, tucking some of my hair behind my ear, then slid behind my neck. Moving so slow I could barely tell, his lips came closer and closer to my own. My hands had found his chest, the hard muscles under the suit and dress shirt flexing of their own accord. It was like waiting for sunrise, just starting to show that first light, building and building, until his lips touched mine, and the explosion occurred.

My fingers slid into his hair, my nails scraping his scalp, as his other hand slid around my waist, pulling me against his hard body. His cock was pressed against my belly, and it wasn't at all where I wanted it. I let out a little mewl, and he took the invitation to dive into my mouth, his tongue sliding against mine, jockeying for power but not overbearing in the least. When he pulled away, I gasped, trying to remember what my lungs were supposed to be used for.

"I need you," I said. "Now."

He didn't hesitate, but grabbed my hand and started marching down the dimly lit hallway. I had no idea where we were going, but I knew I wanted to get there and fast. I didn't want to wait another minute because this guy flipped every damn switch in me so far, and I couldn't wait to see what else he could do to and for me.

CHAPTER SEVEN

L ogan…

She tasted like every fucking wet dream I'd ever had in college, but so much better. Her lips were soft, but she wasn't afraid to take charge, either, and fuck if that didn't just do it for me. When she'd said she needed me, it was all I could do to keep from bending her over right fucking there. It may have been my first time in the stadium, but most of them were laid out the same way. I took an educated guess as to where the visitors' dressing room was. When we crashed through the doors, I thanked every deity that existed, pulling her in behind me.

Turning, I sat on the bench of the closest locker, pulling her down on my lap. Her knees went up on either side of my hips, her shoes falling to the floor. Grabbing her ass, I pressed her against my cock, and she shifted her pelvis to slide along it. Her hands were in my hair, tilting me to get a better angle at my mouth, and I let her take charge.

She feasted at my mouth, her teeth clashing against my own, tongue invading, and I was here for all of it. Some guys I knew would never let a woman be in control, but I'd found that it was much better when both people got what they wanted. I would let her take anything from me because she was doing everything right as far as I was concerned.

When she pulled back, her lips were swollen, her eyes glassy, and she was breathing like she'd just played three minutes straight on the ice.

"I think we've got too many layers between us," she said, her voice husky.

Shifting her weight, she raised herself onto her knees, putting her tits right in my face, and I leaned in and pulled one of her nipples into my mouth. Even with her dress and bra for cushion, she gasped, arching her back, pressing it further in. I bit down a bit, just enough to put pressure, and she sucked a breath in, her body shuddering against me.

"Pants," she said. "And a condom."

"Sure thing," I replied, letting go of her ass and reaching under my own to pull out my wallet.

Thank fuck I had one there 'cause I would not be happy if all this ended up being just a giant fucking tease session. I handed her the condom, then went to work undoing my belt and button. She slid off the bench, taking a step back, a smile on her lips that rivaled any Cheshire cat image I'd ever seen.

"Let me see," she said, licking her lips.

"You just gonna look?" I asked.

"Not what I had planned," she said, holding up the condom in her hand.

"I'm gonna warn you," I said, opening my slacks. "The first round is gonna be quick, so if you want to get yours first, we better get on that."

Biting her lower lip, she looked at me, and the heat was combustible. She had a fire in her eyes that I hadn't seen in entirely too long. Much as I wanted to fuck this woman, I wanted to keep it going after this first time.

"Come here," I said, stalling in my undressing. "Let me get a taste of you, get you riding high."

Swinging her hips, she came closer. I patted the seat

beside me, and she raised her foot, placing it where I'd indicated. Her skirt had a slit that went nearly to her hip, so each side of it went to either side of her thigh, showing me those fucking lace stockings. Slowly, I let my hand slide up her leg, starting at her ankle and heading ever north.

"You wear these cause you wanted someone to see them?" I asked.

"I hate hose," she said. "But I had to wear something with the shoes."

"Well," I said, my hand finally reaching the lace at the top of her stocking. "I rather like them. Question is, do you know how to properly dress with them?"

"Of course," she said. "Gotta be able to get the panties off without taking the whole thing apart."

"Fuck," I said, the word merely a rush of air.

She grabbed the edge of the slit in front of her, lifting it up to reveal a barely there piece of black lace, and sure enough, it was outside the straps for her stockings. It was like she was a wet dream come to life right in the dressing room, and I wasn't gonna let myself miss this opportunity. My hand made it to her hip, and I tugged on the edge of the panties. The flimsy string snapped with just the barest of pressure, like they were meant to be torn off.

"Sorry," I said, looking up at her face.

"It's fine," she replied. "I hated them, anyway."

Taking that as gospel, I took my other hand and snapped the other side, pulling the tiny thing away to reveal gorgeous blonde curls neatly trimmed at the apex of her legs. Tucking the thing that constituted her panties into my jacket pocket, I leaned forward, pulling her closer to me with a hand on either side of her waist.

"You smell like fucking honey," I said, my nose in the curls.

I stuck my tongue out, swiping just at the front of her sex, and she shuddered, flexing her hips, her hands going to my shoulders. Chuckling, I swiped again, and she tilted, opening herself a bit more. It was a bit of a chase, me teasing, her shuddering, and back and forth again. Finally, when she seemed like she was heading higher, she grabbed my head and pushed me further in, my tongue finally finding her opening.

"Mmm," she hummed, her core flexing, her hands fisting in my hair.

Taking one hand off her hip, I slid a finger inside her, and she clenched me so tight I wasn't sure I'd come away fully intact. While my finger slid in and out, my tongue continued to work on her clit, strokes matching the tempo. With her breathing increased and her legs shaking, I was worried she'd collapse, so I pulled the leg on the bench over my shoulder, holding the other tight in my arm. By the time I figured out she was about to fall off that beautiful cliff, I sank my teeth into the tender flesh, holding pressure as she let out a guttural moan that lasted much longer than I thought was possible.

Easing off the pressure and slowing my fingers, I waited as she settled back into herself. When I felt she was steady on her feet, I let go of the leg, allowing her to pull the other from my shoulder. I didn't let her go, just gave her the space to come together.

"Damn," she finally said, her eyes glazed with the afterglow of her orgasm.

"You're welcome," I said, licking her from my lips.

"My turn," she said. The look on my face obviously showed my confusion because she added, "Time for me to get you over the edge."

"Oh, baby," I said. "I'm not done with you yet."

"I'mma need a minute to recover," she said.

"We can't stay in here all night," I replied, pulling her onto my lap. "Much as I'd love to, it wouldn't make the best first impression on my new team."

"You live close by?" she asked.

"Team housing," I replied. "I'll pay for a hotel if you don't want to take me back to your place."

"Hotel works," she replied, moving to stand.

"Not yet," I said, holding her in my lap. "We still got a couple more rounds for you before we make our escape."

CHAPTER EIGHT

Kaia...

He'd literally rocked my world – three times – before he got his. I was still straddling him, though he'd pulled out and had set the condom to the side to dispose of later, when we heard the door open.

"Shit," he mumbled.

"There you are," the man who entered said, a smirk on his face. "Pretty sure, during the meeting, they said to keep our sticks in our pants."

"Shields," Logan said with a sigh that sounded a whole lot like relief. "We missing something?"

"They're wanting to introduce the team," he said. "Players, coaches, owners, the whole nine yards."

"Shit," I said, slipping off his lap, making sure my dress was down and covering everything.

"Might want to check your hair," the other guy said. "And lipstick."

"Fuck," I mumbled, turning to see if I could find a mirror.

Walking through one of the doors on the other side of the locker room, I found a bank of mirrors, and the dude was right. Thankfully, I had my purse still slung over my shoulder, so I pulled out the little comb that was in there and ran it through the messed-up parts of my hair. I pulled the tube of lipstick from the bag and touched that up, too, glad it hadn't smeared across my face.

"Kaia," I heard Logan call.

"Coming," I replied, then snorted a laugh because I'd done that several times already.

"We can't go in together," Logan said, and I nodded. "I'll get you back to the door we came out of so you can slip in there. Shields and I will go to the entrance where the players will be introduced."

"Meet me after?" I asked, because, yeah, I definitely wanted to keep in touch with this guy. He may be a dumb jock, but he was fine in many other ways, as he'd proven in that locker room.

"Here," he said, handing his phone to me. "Add yourself and I'll text you when I'm done."

"Okay," I replied, typing my name and number into the device. I couldn't help but add a couple of emojis so he'd remember who I was and what we'd done. "Here you go," I said, handing it back to him.

He looked down and laughed, saying, "Classy."

"Honest," I replied.

"True," he said.

We'd made it to the convention room, and he went to the door to open it, but before he could, I pulled him to me, giving him a deep kiss.

"Text me," I said, then stepped through the door without a backward glance.

The lights were dimmed somewhat, which I was thankful for, so I slid into a chair at the table I'd been sitting at. Carmen and Nadia were both sitting there, along with Remi, Kylie, and a couple of the other people from our department.

"Where have you been?" Nadia whispered into my ear.

"Indisposed," I said.

"Shit," she muttered. "Were you…"

"Don't say a word," I grumbled under my breath. The last thing I needed was someone to find out I'd been fucking a player in the visiting team's locker room when I was supposed to be schmoozing with everyone else. "I might tell you later," I said, just as the lights dimmed even more.

There was a stage up and to my right where several guys in suits were sitting. I had to assume they were the owners or something because they all looked like businessmen. The owner of Panacea stepped up to the microphone, tapping it to ensure it was on.

"My wonderful employees," Garrett Roberts said. "You all know how much I love sports, and the fact that I was able to join with some of my friends and bring hockey to Seattle has been one of the shining moments in my career. Now, I'm not the only owner because that price tag was just a bit out of my range, so I invited a handful of my friends from college to join me, and here we are.

"You guys are going to be the first to officially meet the team," he continued. "But before we introduce the players, I'd like you to meet the men who jumped with me into this crazy world of the National Hockey League."

Several people clapped, and I joined in. All the stuffed shirts on the stage looked the same. Old business men who had more money than they knew what to do with, so they threw it at a game to try to live out their greatest wishes.

"Some of these men you likely know," the owner continued.

I zoned out, pulling my phone out, hoping to get a text from Logan. Maybe that would distract me enough to make it through the next hour or whatever the stupid speeches would take. Once they got the fuddy-duddies out of the way, they'd get to the real reason most of them were there for. Besides, if Logan texted me, I could pay attention to my phone, sending him ideas for what we could get up to once we were released from the insanity that was this event. Maybe coming to this shindig wasn't such a bad idea after all.

"...Brian Lawrence," the owner said, and I looked up at the stage. "You probably know him from his amazing company, Nectar. At least the ladies will know him."

No!

Of all the people to run into on the other side of the country, he had to show up here and be friends with the owner of the company I worked for. This was like a nightmare come to life.

"Hey," Nadia said, nudging my shoulder. "Your phone's buzzing."

I looked down at it to see a text message from a number I didn't recognize. I opened it up, and thank fuck it was Logan.

> I can't wait to taste you again. The moment we're released, I'm taking you to the closest hotel and fucking your brains out.

Maybe that could make me forget the man standing on the stage.

CHAPTER NINE

Logan...

Standing in line, waiting for the blowhard to finish his speech, I remembered she'd put her number in my phone. If I could have gotten out of the fucking procession of players, I'd've taken her out another exit and found a hotel right away. As it was, I had to listen to this dude go on and on about how much fucking money he had, and how he always wanted to play hockey but couldn't handle it, or his mommy wouldn't let him, or whatever other bullshit excuse he used to make himself feel better.

> I can't wait to taste you again. The moment we're released, I'm taking you to the closest hotel and fucking your brains out.

I saw the little dots show up, letting me know she was typing an answer, only to get a slap on the back from Shields. Looking up, I realized we were heading into the room. It was like we were fucking cattle at auction being sold to the highest bidder, which was something that happened in the lower leagues. God, I hated all the politics that made up being an athlete. Having to go places and do shit you didn't want to do just so the image of the team would be boosted. Well, a fucking lot of good that did me when I ended up getting shipped off to the newest team.

Smiling like they expected, we pranced our happy asses up the couple of steps and onto the stage behind the men with the money. Did they pay us well? Yeah. But that shouldn't mean they owned us. Still, I'd promised my agent I'd play nice, so I was doing what was expected.

I tried to look around the room, but the lights were too low over the tables, and the ones shining on us were too fucking bright. It was worse than when we went on the ice at the beginning of a game. At least then, they didn't shine a fucking spotlight in our faces.

"We have asked that the players stay around and answer questions," the guy who had been talking said. "I'm sure they'll also let you take some selfies with them. Please be responsible when you leave here tonight. If you've enjoyed too much from the bar, use a rideshare to get you home. I don't want to hear that we've lost someone because they didn't plan ahead."

The crowd clapped as the music started back up. All the men in suits stood up and turned to the players. Each one of them shook every player's hand, thanking us for being willing to be on the inaugural roster as if it were our choice. Sometimes, having money made people idiots. But I'd shake their hands and take their checks until I couldn't lace up a pair of skates again.

"YOU'RE JUST SO STRONG," the old woman said, squeezing my bicep. "I bet you get all the girls telling you that, don't you?"

"Sometimes they do," I replied, smiling as her equally ancient friend took a picture.

The two women swapped spots, so the other could get a

picture with me, and it was all good until her hand grabbed my ass. Natural instinct took over, and I sort of slapped the hand away. The look she gave me was equal parts shock and anger.

"We are people," I said. "Asking permission is required."

"There you are," I heard and turned to see Kaia smirking. "I didn't think I'd find you again."

"Here I am," I replied. "If you ladies will excuse me."

"They always go for the pretty girls," one of the women said, her tone anything but polite.

"She probably promised him sex," the other one said, and I had to hold in my laugh because, yeah, she did.

"Thank you," I said, just barely above a whisper.

"I've seen those two," she replied, sliding her hand into the crook of my arm. "They have been known to corner every athlete they come across."

She guided me away from the women and toward the door we'd escaped through before. I was happy to go with her damn near anywhere, but I knew we couldn't leave again, at least not for another half an hour or so.

"I can't stay," she said, looking behind us.

"Why?" I asked, confused.

"I just can't," she said, and the cryptic way she was looking around and talking low made me worried I'd banged a crazy chick.

"I can't leave yet," I said.

"No, I know," she said. "I shouldn't either, but I can't stay here."

"Why?" I asked again.

"It's just…"

She stopped talking, and her eyes widened. I turned to look where she was looking and saw one of the owners walking in our direction.

"Shit," she said before crashing through the door to the hallway.

I wanted to go after her, but I didn't need one of the owners thinking I was just looking to dip my dick, so I turned to look at him.

"Who was that young woman?" he asked.

"No clue," I lied. "She said she wanted to take a picture, but then she ducked through the door."

"I'll have to ask Garrett," he said, and I assumed that was one of the other owners. "Maybe get his employee list and see if she's who I think she is."

"Can a company give a list of employee names to someone outside the company?" I asked. Rich dudes could do whatever the fuck they wanted, but maybe if I gave him a reason why it might not be a good idea, he'd let it go. I could always play the dumb jock angle as to why I'd ask that, but if I could help her out, I would.

"You're right," the guy said, and I was shocked. "Anyway, how have the practices been going?"

"Going good," I said. "We seem like we're coming together nicely. It'll be good to get out there and go for real, though. I see some post-season play in our future."

"I like your attitude," he said, slapping my shoulder. "If the whole team keeps that in mind, we might make history."

"The cup is the ultimate goal," I said, pushing the narrative I'd started. "It's what we all play for."

"True," he said. "Well, glad to have you on board."

"Glad to be here," I replied.

He shook his head like he was trying to forget something, then turned and walked away. I waited until he was far enough away and engaged with someone else to slip through the door and into the hallway. Last thing I needed him to know was I did know the woman, and I was gonna find her.

CHAPTER TEN

K aia...
I was out of breath when I flew through the door to the locker room Logan and I had used earlier, but I couldn't let him see me. If he found me, he might out me, or think he could tell me what to do. Maybe, if I was lucky, I could find another job in another city and start over.

"Damnit," I growled, punching the back of the seat we'd used.

There was no way I was gonna run again. This was just a random fluke, and it wasn't like he'd actually tracked me down. He was here because he was part owner of the team. Did that mean he was moving here? Or was he just here for the initial shit, and then was fucking back off to Minneapolis?

"Shit," I said, realization dawning on me.

The owner of Panacea said they were friends. *Fuck!* Maybe I'd be safe, and he wouldn't ask about me. If he asked some questions, my boss might ask some of his own. No, this was the worst thing that could have happened.

"Kaia," I heard just as Logan came through the door. "Fuck, what was that all about?"

"I can't say," I said. Technically true, since I'd signed an NDA, but I also didn't want to talk about it.

"You know him, don't you," he said. It wasn't a question, so I didn't answer. "Is he dangerous?"

"Not to you," I replied.

"To you, he is, then," he said, and I could see something shift in his eyes. "Did he hurt you?"

"Not in the way you're thinking," I said.

"Because I can take him," he added. "He'd snap like a fucking twig."

"Why do you care?" I asked.

He looked at me, confused for a moment, then sighed.

"Because no one should be afraid," he said. "I'm a protector. It's in my DNA. It's one of the reasons I'm a defenseman. My job is to protect my teammates, especially the goalie. Do you need a protector?"

His question caught me off guard. The explanation of why he cared didn't, but the fact that he asked if I needed to be protected surprised me.

"No one's ever asked me that before," I confessed.

"Then you have shit people in your life," he said. "Tell me if I need to protect you from him."

"I don't know," I said. "I haven't seen him in five years or so. Things were different when I left."

"Is he an ex?" he asked, and I laughed. "Why is that funny?"

"Because there really isn't a way to answer that question," I said.

Someone came through the door, and Logan put himself between me and whoever it was, his body coiled like he was ready to spring at the slightest provocation. Then, just like that, he relaxed.

"Dude," the player who'd come in to warn us about the event said. "You gotta get out of here. They're starting tours of the stadium, and they're gonna get here soon."

"Can we leave?" he asked.

"Maybe," the other guy said. "Check with Coach."

"Come on," he said, turning to me.

I took his hand, but as we headed out the door we'd come in, we could hear the crowd coming. He turned around and damn near dragged me in the other direction, going through the area where I'd checked my makeup, past showers, and doors to offices and equipment rooms until we came out the other side. This hallway was quiet, thank fuck, and we kept walking until we were standing at the other side of the arena near another conference room.

"Here," he said, shoving open the door to the ladies' restroom just outside. "He won't come in here. I'm gonna go find my coach and see if I can leave."

"What are you gonna say?" I asked because I so didn't need this coming back on me.

"That a friend is sick," he said.

"But…"

"It'll be fine," he said. "I'll get you outta here."

"I don't want you to get into trouble," I said.

"I've been in trouble my whole life," he said. "I'm kind of an expert at it. Trust me."

He looked into my eyes like he was begging me to believe him. I nodded, he kissed me, then was out the door before I even registered what was happening. Pulling my phone out, I sent a text to Nadia telling her I had a headache and was going home.

Suuuuure.

Of course, she wouldn't believe me. Whatever. I just muted my phone but watched the chat with Logan. I just hoped I wasn't jumping from the frying pan into the fire.

CHAPTER ELEVEN

Logan...

It took a while, but I finally figured out how to get back to the home team dressing room, which is where I found my coach. The look he gave me when I walked through the door told me he'd noticed my absence but wasn't gonna give me any shit about it, which was a good thing.

"Thanks for joining us, Knox," he said.

"Sorry," I said. "Was helping a guest who was sick."

"Sure," he said, and some of the guys snickered. "Whatever you were doing, it's done now."

"No," I said. "I gotta take her to the urgent care down the road. She's not doing well but said she didn't want to take an ambulance. I'm afraid she's gonna get dehydrated or something."

His arms folded over his chest said he didn't buy anything I was selling. Finally, he sighed and said, "This is your one get-outta-trouble moment. Don't pull this shit after today. Got it?"

"Yes, sir," I said. "I really am worried about her."

"Get," he barked. "Before I change my mind."

I didn't have to be told twice, so I turned on my heel and

headed out the door. Walking back the way I'd come, I pulled out my phone to send a text to her to let her know I was on my way back. I got near the restroom I'd shoved her in, only to come up on the crowd that was doing the tour coming right at me. I ducked into the men's room, sliding into a stall and shutting the door.

"I don't know," I heard the same man from earlier say as he entered the space. "All I know is that I'm sure it's her and she might be working for Garrett."

I didn't hear another side of the conversation, so he must have been talking on the phone. As far as I could tell, he was the only one who came into the bathroom, so he likely wouldn't be overheard. Staying as quiet as I could, I listened to see if I could figure out what this dude's problem was and why Kaia was avoiding him.

"That's just it," he said, continuing his conversation. "He doesn't know who she is or what she did to me. If it's her, I can't let her talk to Garrett. He'd pull me from the team's ownership at the very least."

There was another pause, but he hummed an agreement of some kind. Whatever it was, it wasn't good. If he didn't even want his friend to know who she was, maybe she wasn't as innocent as I thought. Still, she was truly scared when she saw him coming toward her.

"I'm still looking for her," he said. "If I find her, I won't be letting her go. Not again. She needs to atone for what she did. That's the least I expect from her."

Nothing this guy was saying made sense to me. I wanted to go out and slam him against the wall, demanding he tell me everything, but I didn't think that would help her. At least, not right away. That moment might come, but for now, I was gonna just keep myself quiet and listen in. Maybe he'd say something that would give me a direction to look.

"Look," he said. "I gotta keep looking. If she's here, I'll find her. There are only so many places she can hide. I'll call you back when I get her, and we can figure out how to go from there."

I heard the door to another stall open, so I peeked through the crack between the door and the frame, but couldn't see shit. I didn't want to leave and have him see me, so I stayed put. I did send a text to Kaia to let her know that the guy was looking for her, so she should stay put and hide. The other toilet flushed, and I heard the stall door open. Then I heard the door out of the room open and close. Of fucking course, he wouldn't wash his hands. Some guys just didn't get it.

When I left the stall, the restroom was vacant, so I walked over to the door, praying the dude had left the area. Cracking open the door, I saw the corridor was empty, so I stepped out and walked the few steps to the ladies' room.

"Hello," I said as I pushed the door open. Nothing but silence greeted me, so I went in, praying Kaia was still there. "Kaia? You in here? It's Logan."

"Oh, thank fuck," she said. The distinct sound of shoes hitting the ground greeted me, and when the far-end stall opened, she looked scared and pissed in equal measure. "Whatever you heard, it's lies."

Her conviction was there in the words she said, and I wondered what she'd gotten mixed up with when it came to that dude.

"We can talk about it later," I said, grabbing her hand. "For now, let's get you the fuck outta here."

The door to the restroom opened, and I held my breath, but it was the woman who had come up to us at the table earlier.

"Oh my God," she said, looking between me and Kaia. "I knew you were screwing around. I mean, I can't blame you, but still."

"Carmen," Kaia said. "Someone's here who's a danger to me. I need to get out of here. Logan's gonna help me, but can

43

you cover if anyone asks? Just say you saw me throwing up in the bathroom or something."

"Yeah, that," I said. "I told the coach I was taking a sick woman to urgent care."

"You guys are just gonna go find a hotel or something, aren't you?" she asked.

"Whatever," Kaia said. "You can believe whatever you want, but I really do have to leave without anyone knowing where I'm going."

"So," she said, blocking our way out. "Who's this dangerous guy?"

"I can't tell you," Kaia said.

"You probably can't tell me why he's dangerous, either, can you?"

"No," Kaia said. "Look, I trust you, but this is above your pay grade, and I don't want to put you in any danger. You are either gonna trust me or not. Don't really care. But move so I can leave."

Something must have been clear in her begging, because Carmen's demeanor changed dramatically. "You really are scared," she said. "Like, really scared."

"Yeah," Kaia said, the word coming out almost on a sob.

"Okay," Carmen said. "Let me check the hallway, then I'll tell everyone you were sick and went to get checked out. I can even say I'm not feeling great, that maybe it's food poisoning or something."

"Thank you," Kaia said, her relief clear in her voice.

Carmen opened the door, looked both ways, then ushered us out. She walked with us along the corridor until we got somewhere that we could get out of the building. Slipping into the warm September night, I tucked Kaia into my body as we went toward the parking lot.

"I got you," I said against the top of her head. "I'll keep you safe."

CHAPTER TWELVE

K aia...

"I got you," he said. "I'll keep you safe."

His words were soothing, but I wouldn't feel safe until I was well and truly away from Brian Lawrence. My past was just that, the past. No reason why it needed to come back to bite me in the ass. Although, I figured at some point it would.

I'd finally found myself feeling like I'd escaped the flaws of my life's choices, of the demons I'd decided to lay with to get me ahead. Now, though, that demon had slithered back into my sphere of existence. If life were fair, I'd have never seen him again. Life wasn't fair, though, and tonight was just another example of that reality.

"Here," he said, opening the passenger door of a modest sedan. "I'll get you to a hotel. Whether we do anything else doesn't matter."

The man was a contradiction walking because he'd been hot to get me to a bed and have his way with me again.

"You got more condoms?" I asked him as he slid behind the wheel. He looked at me, eyes showing concern and desire, then shook his head. "Then we stop at a store and pick some up. I'm gonna need some serious distractions tonight."

He only paused a moment before starting the car and pulling out of the lot. Downtown was busy, with it being a Friday night, but he maneuvered us through it like a pro, slipping into the valet for one of the high-rise hotels near the arena. The doorman opened my door, but Logan was there before I had my seatbelt undone.

"Did you forget a stop?" I asked as he handed his keys over.

"There is such a thing as delivery," he said with a smile. "Don't need them immediately."

"Says you," I replied.

We walked into the lobby and went up to the front desk.

"Room for the night?" the clerk asked.

"Yes," Logan said.

"Do you have any preferences?"

"Just a bed," he said. "Do you have a store or can I have something delivered?"

"No onsite store," she said. "But delivery is fine. Just make sure you give them your room number so I'll know who to call when it arrives."

"Great," he said. "If you have a king, that would be preferable. Better yet, if you've got a suite, we'll take that."

"Let me check," she said. "Just tonight?"

He looked at me and I shrugged.

"Let's make it two," he said, pulling me closer to him.

"We have one suite available," she said. "It's $1,150 a night." My eyes nearly popped out of my head, but he just pulled out a card and set it on the counter.

"Do you have a car?"

"It's with the valet," he said.

"Any luggage?"

"No," he said.

She did whatever she needed to do to get the room for us,

then swiped his card and pulled out a sheet for him to complete. Once that was done, she handed us the key cards and directions to the elevators. When we got in and the doors closed, I looked at him.

"This is an awfully expensive splurge," I said. "That's like my rent for the month."

"You're worth it," he said, kissing me on the forehead.

The elevators opened and we walked down the hall until we found our room. He pressed the key card on the lock mechanism on the door, the green light popped up, and he pushed the door open, flicking on the light. The room was bigger than my apartment, but what really drew me in were the floor-to-ceiling windows directly in front of me.

I was drawn toward them, maneuvering around the sofa and chairs, dropping my purse into one of them before I was standing in front of the glass, looking out over Elliott Bay. His arms slid around me, his body pressing against my back.

"I placed an order," he said, kissing the shell of my ear. "We've got about half an hour until it gets here."

Turning in his arms, I wrapped my own around his neck, stretching up to press my lips to his. He responded in kind, moving me back against the window. The chill of the glass countered the heat of his body, and his hands roamed down to my ass, pulling my leg up and onto his hip. His arousal was flush against my core, pressing hard against the folds he'd played earlier in the night.

We both jumped when my phone went off.

"Ignore it," he growled against my lips, pressing his cock against me.

The phone stopped but started right back up again. I pretended it didn't exist until it went off again and then again.

"Fuck," I said, shifting from his grasp.

Pulling the phone from my purse, I looked at the screen

that read, *Private Number*. The ringing stopped but then started once again.

"Hello?" I asked when I answered it.

"Hello, Kaia," he said. "Did you think I wouldn't find you?"

"Leave me alone," I said, and I hated that my voice sounded weak.

"But you owe me so much," he continued. "You can try to hide, but I'll always find you."

Logan was at my back, his arm around my waist, as he took the phone from me.

"Lady said to leave her alone," he said into the phone. There was a pause, and then he said, "Good luck with that." He disconnected the call, then shut it off before dropping it on the chair with my purse. "Hey," he said, his finger under my chin, tipping it up. "I won't let anything happen to you."

"You don't know him," I said, barely holding back a sob.

"Don't need to," he replied. "All those rich assholes think they can throw their money at a problem, and it'll go away. Or that they can get whatever they want, simply by buying it."

"Trust me," I said, but he silenced me with a kiss.

His lips pressed against mine, his arms wrapping around my waist, and his tongue sliding along the seam of my lips until I let him in. Everything in me was trying desperately to figure out how to save myself. When he backed me through the door to the bedroom and to the bed, pressed me down on the mattress, and hiked my leg up over his hip, my brain shut off, and all I could think about was this man who was with me, seemed unafraid of the big bad wolf that could come knocking at the door at any minute.

CHAPTER THIRTEEN

L ogan...

She was terrified of whoever this man was. Truth be told, if he had the money, he could do whatever the fuck he wanted. That wasn't something she needed to know, though. Instead. she needed to be redirected in a much more pleasurable direction, one I was happy to assist with. If I could fuck her until she couldn't remember her name, maybe then she'd tell me who he was and what hold he had over her.

The ringing phone on the nightstand drew my attention away from the soft woman beneath me.

"Mr. Knox?" the woman on the other end said.

"Yes," I replied.

"Your order has arrived at the front desk," she said. "Would you like me to have someone bring it up for you?"

"Please," I said. "The sooner the better, too."

"Of course," she replied, and the forced politeness in her voice clued me in to the fact that I was rude.

"Sorry," I apologized. "I just forgot to get some things before we got here."

"Completely understandable," she replied. "Will there be anything else?"

"I don't think so," I said.

"Have a good evening," she said before hanging up.

"Don't move," I said to Kaia.

I got up and headed toward the door. Pulling it open, I waited. The elevator doors opened, and someone in a suit walked out and toward me. As he came up to me he smiled and handed over the bag.

"Need anything else?" he asked.

"Nope," I replied, slapping a hundred-dollar bill in his hand. "Except to be left alone," I added.

"Of course," he said, and it was clear he knew what was in the bag and what was going to be happening for the next few hours.

Closing the door, I threw the deadbolt and flipped the extra security thing before turning to head back into the bedroom. When I walked in, the bed was empty, but the door to the bathroom was closed. Opening the bag, I pulled the box of condoms out and set them on the nightstand. I'd also gotten a bottle of wine, some chocolate, and whipping cream. There may have been an ulterior motive behind my choices, but that didn't matter.

Knocking on the bathroom door, I said, "Hey."

"Give me a minute?" she asked.

"Sure," I said. "Whenever you're ready, everything's good to go."

"Okay," she said.

I heard the water turn on, then the spray of the shower. Guess she was gonna clean up before we got dirty, which was fine by me. While she was in there, I pulled my jacket off and put it on the chair near the window. Next was the tie, as I kicked my shoes off, and then the shirt. I had a tee shirt underneath, so I left that on, along with my slacks, but I pulled my keys and wallet from my pockets, setting them on top of the clothes.

When the water finally turned off, I sighed. The door opened and steam billowed out. Girl liked a hot shower, I guessed. She was wrapped in a white, terrycloth robe, cinched at the waist. Her hair was damp around the edges, but that was the only indication she'd actually been under the spray.

"We're gonna have to share a shower," she said.

"Let's get dirty first," I replied, standing from the edge of the bed.

The sway of her hips drew my eyes, and she sashayed her very fine ass toward me. Much as I wanted to pull the cord holding the robe together, I wanted to see what she was gonna do, first. Stopping in front of me, just barely out of reach, she leaned to the side toward the nightstand. I followed her motion as she picked up the whipping cream.

"This for me or you?" she asked.

"Us," I replied, my cock straining to be released.

Her smile turned wicked, light dancing in her eyes, and I was glad that something had pulled her out of whatever funk she'd found herself in. Now, I just needed to make sure she forgot it completely.

CHAPTER FOURTEEN

K aia...

Pulling the sash of the robe, I let it fall open, then fall from my shoulders. Logan sat perfectly still, but his eyes caressed my skin just as much as his hands had in that locker room. I could feel the way they slid along my skin, and I reveled in it.

Taking the top off the whipped cream, I shook the can to get it ready to go, then tipped it up and let some of the cream out along the top of my breast. It started to slide down, and by the time I'd sprayed the other one, it was nearly ready to drip onto the floor.

"You better get that," I said, setting the can back on the nightstand. "Pretty sure they'll charge you extra if they have to clean the carpets."

He took the invitation, coming up off the bed in an instant, his lips sliding along the bottom of my breast, cleaning up the white fluff. The heat from his tongue as he lapped it up, then circled my nipple, made my knees weak, but his hands found my hips to hold me up. He gave the same treatment to the other breast, cleaning up the mess I'd made with the can of cream.

"Come on," he said, turning me back toward the bathroom. "Let's make use of that shower you were talking about."

I heard his clothes hit the floor as we walked into the large space. Heading to the shower, he gave a low whistle, and I turned to look at him.

"Damn," he said. "I might have to extend our stay."

Laughing, I stepped into the large shower and turned the faucet on. The space was almost as big as my whole bathroom in my apartment, and there was a clawfoot tub nestled at one end of it, while shower heads were scattered around the perimeter. The one in the ceiling wouldn't come on until you pulled one of the levers on the side.

His body pressed against my back, his cock sliding along my ass, his hands coming in front of me, one heading north, the other south, and he pulled me back against him. Lips pressed against my neck as his fingers slid down between my thighs. His other hand firmly held my breast, my nipple sliding between his finger and thumb. I let out a throaty moan as he found the bundle of nerves at the apex of my sex.

"That's it," he whispered in my ear. "Let the world fall away and just enjoy yourself."

His words had the exact opposite effect that I'm sure he wanted them to because my eyes popped open and I stiffened.

"What's wrong?" he asked, still holding me but keeping his hands still.

"I need to tell you something," I said. "I don't want to, but I need to."

"Hey," he said, turning me in his arms. "You don't owe me any explanation. Whoever that asshole is, he can't hurt you anymore. I can protect you."

"You don't understand," I said, and my throat squeezed. "He owns me."

CHAPTER FIFTEEN

L ogan...

"He owns me," she said.

"You can't own someone," I said. "It's not legal."

She didn't say anything. Honestly, I didn't think she could. Her eyes were wide, tears filling them, and she was shaking. Shit, she was having a panic attack. I pulled her from the shower and into the bedroom, picking up the robe and wrapping it around her. Settling her on the edge of the bed, she seemed wooden, like her soul had been sucked from the husk that was her body.

"Hey," I said, crouching in front of her. "What can I do?"

She blinked like she was coming out of some sort of trance or something. Tears spilled down her cheeks, but other than that, she hadn't really made any movement I didn't initiate. Finally, after entirely too long, she let out a sob, her hand going to her mouth before another came out and then another.

I was on the bed, her on my lap, my arms wrapped around her before the next one came, and she fell apart. Her body shook from the ferocity of her sobs, gasping for air, then letting it all out again. It was heartbreaking to feel and hear, and all I wanted to do was make it go away, but I didn't know how.

When she had cried herself out and her body was relaxed, I leaned back a bit, trying to look at her face. She was limp in my arms, her breathing even, and I realized she'd fallen asleep. Much as I wanted to get off, I knew this was neither the time nor the place for that to happen. Instead, I shifted her onto the bed, hoping to get her tucked in so I could take care of myself. Unfortunately, she wouldn't let go of me, so I was forced to join her. It wasn't really a hardship to hold her, though, and before long, I was drifting off myself.

CHAPTER SIXTEEN

K aia…

Taking a deep breath, I felt his arms tighten around my body, and I froze. My brain tried desperately to remember where I was and, more importantly, who I was with. Piecing things together, I remembered Logan, the way he'd played my body like an instrument in the locker room. That's when I remembered Brian Lawrence was there, too.

Using the breathing exercises my therapist had given me years ago, I focused on the in and out of taking breaths until my heart slowed down and I was a bit more in control. The grip Logan had on me wasn't gonna let me loose, so I settled myself back in against him, feeling the morning rise in his cock. We'd lost an entire night because of my fucked-up brain, but I wouldn't let the rest of our time in this fancy hotel go to waste.

Shifting my hips, I ground my ass against his cock. The groan from him made me smile. His hand slid up my body, cupping my breast in it, sliding along my sensitive nipples. The rough skin on his palm pebbled them, straining against it for more friction. I slid my hand lower in an attempt to get things going for myself.

In a motion that would only happen with someone who had a mastery of their body, he slid me onto my back, blocked my hand, and slid his own down to my core. His thick fingers sliced through my folds, pressing along my seam until he found purchase and plunged in, drawing a gasp from me.

"You're so wet," he mumbled, his mouth by my ear. "Wet and tight. You're a fucking dream come true."

The palm of his hand rubbed against my clit, the roughness just the stimulation I needed, and the faster he pumped his fingers in and out of me, the faster that palm scraped along those nerves until everything exploded in fireworks behind my eyelids, thunder rolling through my veins until every nerve ending was engulfed in the inferno of my orgasm.

"Damn," he said, sliding his body over mine. "Do it again."

He slid his cock against my entrance and I tensed.

"It's covered," he said. "I'm not that stupid."

I relaxed a bit, opening my legs more to allow his hips between me better. Tilting my pelvis, he slid in, pressing his body against mine.

"Mmm," he hummed.

He stayed still for a minute or two before slowly shifting his hips up and away from me. Then, with a swift thrust, he shoved back in, the head of his cock sliding right along the rough patch at the front of my pussy. With how worked up he'd gotten me, it didn't take but a couple more thrusts, and I was riding that edge again.

"Come on," he growled, pumping in and out. "I want you to lose yourself again. Let go. Let me make you feel good."

His words weren't doing what he thought they were. No doubt, they worked on most people, but I couldn't lose control, at least not in the way he wanted me to. Instead of telling him to shut up, I pulled his head down and captured his lips, thrusting my tongue into his mouth at the same rhythm he was thrusting his cock into my pussy. The more I sped up, the more he did until I'd forgotten whatever it was that he'd been saying and let my body take over, exploding again. He pulled away, slamming into me until he stiffened, his arms shaking as he came. When he collapsed, he was kind enough to do it off to the side and not directly on me.

"Damn," he said, mimicking the word he'd used earlier.

"Yeah," I agreed.

Sliding out of me, he held the condom at the root of his cock until he was free, then pulled it off and set it on top of the comforter.

"Shower or bath?" he asked as he shifted on the bed.

"Bath," I said. "But we need food first."

"On the way," he said. "I kinda just ordered some of everything, not knowing what you might want."

"When did you have time to do that?" I asked, completely confused.

"Middle of the night," he said with a shrug. "I woke up to pee, you were sleeping well, so I called the desk to see about some room service. They set it up to be delivered late enough to not wake us up but early enough to give us stamina for the rest of the day."

"My God, you're not an idiot," I said.

He smiled this sort of cocky, lopsided thing that made him absolutely adorable. I reached a hand out, caressing his cheek, and pulled him to me. The kiss was slow and sensuous, nothing like the other ones we'd shared, and I reveled in it. There was a knock at the door that interrupted us.

"There's the food," he said as he pulled back. "Be right back."

He grabbed the robe from the floor and tried to pull it on, but there was no way it would fit around his broad shoulders. Laughing, I leaned over, found a towel that had been dropped there, and threw it at him. He snagged it from the air with ease, then turned to head out of the bedroom. I had to admit that watching him leave was definitely a perk of this little piece of insanity I found myself in.

When he was out of sight, I slid off the edge of the bed, grabbed the used rubber he'd left, and headed into the bathroom. Dropping the condom into the trash can, I stepped into the little room where the toilet was and shut the door. After I'd relieved myself, I washed my hands and looked in the mirror. The dark circles that had been a constant under my eyes when I was in Minnesota were threatening to come back.

"Hey," Logan said behind me.

"Is that bacon I smell?"

"Sure is," he said, a smile across his face. "Eggs, bacon, sausage, coffee, toast, pancakes…"

"Damn," I said, mimicking the words he'd said earlier. "You buy the whole restaurant?"

"Didn't know what you'd want," he said. "Can't have you hungry with all I've got planned for the day."

I raised my eyebrows at him and he laughed, which released whatever tension I'd had in me as I joined him.

"Come on," he said. "I wanna watch you eat a sausage."

CHAPTER SEVENTEEN

L ogan...
    She ate like she'd been starved, and I wondered how many secrets she had. She knew one of the owners, and intimately, if I had to guess. The way she used her body and the unabashed way she enjoyed me using it told me she wasn't a stranger to sex. What I didn't know, was this thing she kept saying about being owned. It didn't sit right with me, but I didn't want to push her away, so I tried to pretend she hadn't said anything.

"You don't seem to like me talking to you during sex," I said, having polished off much more than I should have. "Why's that?"

"Just don't see a point," she said, and I watched her walls go up.

I had just under a week until camp started in earnest. They'd made sure we showed up for the shindig last night, but we were free for the rest of the weekend and into the first part of the next week. I'd originally planned to use it to see the sites around my new home city, but now I wanted to spend the entire time with Kaia.

"You saying my mouth should be busy doing something

else?" I asked, hoping to lighten the mood that had darkened her eyes.

"Something like that." she said.

Picking up a sausage link in her fingers, she brought it up to her lips, a smile sliding along them as she stuck her tongue out and licked the entire length of it. It was tiny, really, but the eroticism wasn't lost on me or my cock, which reacted as if she were doing to it what she was doing to the breakfast food. Opening her mouth, she slid it in, her tongue sliding along the bottom of it as she slid it all the way in, and damn if I didn't want to replace that with myself.

"What?" she asked after she'd chewed and swallowed.

"Pretty sure we need to put that mouth to use in other ways," I said, my hand on my cock, stroking it under the table.

"That a fact?" she asked, arching her back so her bare breasts were thrust out, begging for attention. "Your mouth is doing a hell of a lot more talking than it should."

"Come here," I said, sliding the chair back from the table.

Standing up, she grabbed a packet of syrup from the table before coming to me. I reached out to grab her, but she backed up and shook her head, her smile wicked with intent. Holding my hands up in surrender, I sat back on the chair, unsure what she had in mind but desperate to find out. She looked around and seemed to think better of whatever she had in mind. She grabbed my hand to pull me up, then turned and headed into the bedroom and through it to the bathroom until she was standing in the shower.

"Sit," she said, pointing to the small seat on the side of the shower.

Following her direction, I did as she asked. The tile was fucking cold, but I would sit on an ice block if it meant she'd pay attention to me. Stepping up to me, she slid between my knees, opened the packet, and then tipped it up, letting the sticky, sweet concoction drip along her breasts before tipping it back up. Since she was in charge of things right now, I waited for her to tell me what she wanted me to do.

"Clean this up," she said, her tone a mix of desire and demand.

Leaning forward, I pulled one of her nipples into my mouth, the syrup sweetening her natural flavor. Her back arched and she sighed. As her hands went to my shoulders, mine went to her waist, my fingers digging into her flesh. I moved to the other breast, giving it the same attention I gave the first.

When the syrup was fairly cleaned up, I let my hand slide down along her thigh, my thumb sliding through the curls to her clit, where I began to work it in circles. As if I'd pressed a button, her legs opened, allowing me better access to her. I let my fingers find her opening, sliding in first one, then a second, until her grip on my shoulders tightened and her core squeezed around my digits.

"Yeah," she said, her breath coming faster.

Not wanting to throw her off track, I kept my mouth shut and just let her feel, continuing my pumping in and out of her. My thumb circled her clit, and she clenched, her stomach spasming as her orgasm overtook her. When her body slowed, I pulled my fingers out and pulled her onto my lap, my arms wrapping around her.

"That was amazing," she said. "But I need you to get yours, too."

"We got time," I said.

"I'm sticky," she said. "And I haven't gotten that bath."

"Come on," I said, standing up with her. "I got something for that, too."

I walked her over to the tub, turning the tap on to warm the water. Plugging the drain, I helped her in, then went back out to the bedroom where the bag from the store I'd ordered from the night before was. Shuffling through the contents, I found the bath bomb. Unwrapping it, I went back into the bathroom and let it slide into the water with her.

"Join me?" she asked.

"In a minute," I replied.

Going back to the bedroom, I grabbed a couple of condoms to take with me, just in case we got to a point to need them. When I got back into the bathroom, her eyes were closed, and the foam was rising. She looked relaxed, and I hated to disturb her. Sitting on the edge of the tub, I just watched as she let the water lap over her.

CHAPTER EIGHTEEN

K aia...

"I can hear you," I said.

"You're beautiful," he said.

I heard him shift, then felt the water slosh as he got into the tub. His leg slid along the outside of mine as he settled, then I felt him shift again. Opening my eyes, I looked at him, trying to figure out how much I could trust him. He'd been kind, had kept me safe from Brian, and had brought me to amazing heights. Still, my secrets were much bigger than he could even imagine.

"Come here," he said, reaching out.

Shifting, I turned myself around so my back was to his front, his legs outside my own. Leaning back against his chest, I felt him give a little sigh, and wasn't quite sure what to think about that. By the time the water got up and nearly over my breasts, he reached back and turned it off. It was quiet, just the sound of the water sloshing a bit as it settled and our breathing. Closing my eyes again, I relaxed into him, his arms around my waist. As much as I'd loved the sex, this was just what I needed to get my mind off the night before.

"I know you don't want to talk about it," he said, his voice low next to my ear. "But I'm afraid I'm gonna need to know if the owner you know will make problems for me or for you."

I knew the question was going to come at some point, but wasn't sure how it was going to be asked. The fact that he made it about him, not me, was kinda nice. Either he'd dealt with jealous exes or knew what kind of man Brian was. Whichever it was, it had to be hashed out, and now was as good a time as any.

"I worked for him," I said, my voice low to match his. "Not in the way one normally works for someone. Not how I work at Panacea now. This was something that was forced on me, and as much as I hate it, is still haunting me."

His arms tightened around me, and he kissed the top of my shoulder. Taking a moment to steady myself, I started again, telling him the story of my life with every detail spelled out clearly. To his credit, he didn't flinch, argue, try to cover for the dude, or anything like that. He asked a couple of clarifying questions but otherwise just listened.

"That's heavy," he said once I'd finished. "I feel like I should apologize for everything you went through."

"It's been years," I said. "I'm mostly okay now."

"Still," he said, and I felt him shrug and sigh. "How did he find you?"

"No clue," I replied. "I've been very careful. I've had to be."

"Sounds like he's friends with the guy who owns the company you work for," he said. "Do you think that's how he found you?"

"I don't think so," I said. "Mr. Roberts is a really great guy. Very respectful of all of us. If he's the one who told Brian, I feel like I would have felt that was coming. The company is extremely careful about employee information. We do security software and products alongside all the other things we offer. It was a big reason I came here. That, and it was over sixteen-hundred miles away from where I lived."

"How long have you been out here?" he asked. "And you don't have to answer any of my questions. I'm just trying to figure this out."

"I've been here for five years," I said. "That's why I thought I was safe. The random connection to the owner of my company and the fact that he showed up to an event I was at – one I likely would never have gone to if given a choice – makes me really confused."

"Well," he said, giving another squeeze. "I'll keep you safe. I don't know how, but I will. What are you gonna do when you have to go back to work?"

"I work from home," I said. "Not always, but often. I think I can pull off a week of being at home, what with me having left the party because I was 'sick' and all. After that, though, I'm not sure."

"Do you think he can figure out where you live?"

I shuddered because this guy could find damn near anything. He'd figured out my phone number, which meant he had access to at least some information about me. If it was through Panacea, I would have to quit and run again. After finally feeling like my past was truly that, to pick up and run again would just suck. That, and it would prove that he really could find me anywhere.

"I can stay with you," he said, obviously sensing my unease. "If you want, I mean."

Tilting my head to the side, I looked up at him. The honesty in his eyes, the way he was looking at me like I actually fucking mattered more than just what my body could do, damn near broke my heart. Why couldn't I have found him back when this whole thing started? Maybe then I wouldn't have ended up in such a fucked-up situation that I had to run from.

CHAPTER NINETEEN

L ogan...

What a fucking nightmare this woman had been through. The fact that she wasn't locked up in a padded room was a testament to her strength of character, not to mention her mental capabilities. Fuck, just listening to it was rough. We'd talked for quite a while in the tub until the water started to get cold. Then, I got her out, dried her off, and then took her to bed.

She was relaxed, and I wondered whether she was going to crash like she had the night before. Instead, she pulled me down on top of her, her body soft and warm. With her hands and her mouth, she told me what she wanted me to do, and I was more than willing. The slow, sensual sex we shared would likely be classified as making love, but I didn't want to give it that name. I wasn't sure how long this situation would last, but for as long as she wanted me, I would be here for her.

When I woke a few hours later, she wasn't in bed. I worried that she'd slipped out, maybe that she'd played me and taken off with my wallet or something. It would serve me right for being as open as I was with what I had with me, splurging on an expensive hotel room, and just flat-out giving and giving to her. Then I heard her talking. I couldn't make out what she was saying, but she was speaking to someone. Since I only heard her voice, I assumed she was talking on the phone.

"...so I'm not gonna make it into the office," she said as I stepped out of the bedroom. "No," she continued, oblivious to my presence. "I'm sure it's nothing, but I don't want to share it with anyone if it's contagious."

Watching her on the phone, sitting at the table, the robe she'd been using wrapped around her, I wondered if she was really not feeling well or if this was about the man she was trying to avoid.

"Thanks, Remi," she said, then disconnected the call, setting her phone on the table.

I waited, watching her to see if she did anything else, but she just sighed and then put her head down on her arms on the table.

"Hungry?" I asked, and she jumped.

"Shit," she said, a hand to her chest. "You scared the ever-loving shit outta me."

"Sorry," I said, walking to the table to sit next to her. "Do you want me to order room service?"

"I should probably eat," she said.

"We worked up an appetite in the last few hours," I said. "Let's figure out what's good."

"Honestly," she said. "I'd really like to go somewhere. I'm feeling a bit cooped up here."

"You aren't afraid someone will see you?" I asked.

"Nah," she said. "We can find something to wear that will keep us under the radar."

"You've got that dress," I said. "And I've got that fucking monkey suit. We'd have to either order something or swing by our places. Besides, I'm not wearing those shoes all day. They hurt like a motherfucker."

"I got you," she said, turning her phone over and pressing apps and whatever. "What size shoes do you wear?" she asked.

"Ten," I said. "But you don't need to get me shoes."

"Hush," she said, her smile growing. She looked at me, clicked a few things, then back at me again. I had no idea what she was doing, but it was weird that she was just looking at me, then selecting things. "Okay," she said after she set her phone back down. "We should have something here within a couple of hours. Until then, I'm gonna take a quick shower. You're free to join me if you want."

With that, she stood up, pulled the tie around her waist, and let the robe drop on the chair. As she walked by, she leaned down, her hand sliding down my chest to my cock, which had definitely stood up to pay attention, gave me a squeeze and a tug, kissed me, then walked by. Fuck if I didn't follow her like she'd been holding a leash.

The condoms I'd brought in when we were in the bath were still sitting on the little shelf next to it. She grabbed a couple of towels and tossed them over the bar just outside the shower, taking a washcloth and hand towel in with her. When the water started running, she turned to me, dropped the hand towel on the ground, fiddled with it, then kneeled down on it and looked up through her lashes.

I stood there like a fucking moron until she crooked her finger at me, a come hither motion with her hand and the same look in her eyes. She'd situated herself so she was under the spray, but the bench was near to where she was. Walking over, I stopped in front of her, my back to the bench. When I went to sit down, she wrapped her arms around my legs to keep me up. Guess she wanted to do things her way, and I was definitely happy to oblige.

Her tongue slipped out of her mouth, licking the underside of my cock, from base to tip, giving a bit of a swirl around the end before pulling it into her mouth. It slid all the fucking way in, and that was saying something. Not that I wanted to toot my own horn, but I was big, as in long and thick. I'd never had anyone be able to take all of me in their mouth, but she did. It was like her gag reflex had been broken or something.

That thought did the opposite of what I had wanted, and she pulled off me and looked up, confused.

"It's not you," I said. "Trust me. Just thinking back to our talk, which is not where my mind should be."

"I can stop," she said.

"Only if you want to," I said. "You're in control. You do what you want, and I'll respond accordingly."

As if my words had some sort of magic power or some-thing, she smiled, her entire face brightening, and she went back to her task, sucking cock like it was her favorite thing in the world. I closed my eyes, banishing all thoughts of her past from my brain, and just let myself feel the way she was worshipping me, and damn if that didn't do the trick. It didn't take long at all for me to get that feeling – the tingling at the base of my spine, the tightening of my balls, the throb-bing in my cock – culminating in my body going rigid, my hand reaching out for the wall to keep me upright, and Kaia sliding a finger into my ass as I exploded into her mouth.

"Holy fuck," I breathed out when my body remembered it was supposed to do that. "I have never…"

"Was that okay?" she asked, looking up from her kneeling position.

"More than," I replied. I sat on the bench, pulling her into my lap. "You are amazing. I don't know what your plans are going forward, but I will be happy to take care of you in whatever capacity you want."

"You haven't even known me a full day," she said.

"Don't care," I replied. "We can fly to Vegas and get hitched, then come back, and you won't have to worry about the asshole from your past."

She looked down, but I caught the look in her eyes before they darted away.

Fuck.

CHAPTER TWENTY

K aia...
First, I couldn't put him in the kind of position he was asking of me. Brian was partial owner of the team he played for. A team, he admitted, was his last-ditch effort to stay in the league. If they canned him because of me, it would kill me. I couldn't do that to him. Second, there was the small problem of marriage, of which I currently wasn't eligible to do.

"What is it?" he asked.

"It's complicated," I said. "But it's something I think I'm ready to figure out. If you wouldn't mind helping me, that is."

I hated to ask for more from this man, but he was here, he'd heard my story, and he hadn't gone running screaming. Maybe, just maybe, this was the time to get right with myself.

"Say the word," he said.

"Word," I replied, and he smiled this big, goofy grin that just melted my cold, dead heart. "I take it from that look you'll help?"

"Where do we start?" he asked.

"I should probably find an attorney," I said. "I mean, there are things that will have to be ironed out, contracts that have to be dealt with."

"I know a guy," he said. "But before we do that, can I do something for you?"

I didn't get a chance to answer because the hotel room phone started ringing.

"Hold that thought," he said, standing up but shifting me to sit back on the bench we'd been on.

While he was gone, I took the time to clean myself up, washing my hair quickly. He joined me not too long after, taking over the task of cleaning my body, and he did it thoroughly, ensuring that every inch of me was squeaky clean. I was also given an orgasm during the process, which is never a bad thing. When a knock sounded on the hotel room door, we'd finished the washing, and he walked out with a towel around his waist to open it while I continued to dry off.

"You can't go in there," Logan shouted, and I went into the room with the toilet, locking the door.

"I know you're in here," I heard Brian say, his fucking voice like a nightmare come to life. "You couldn't hide from me for long, you know. I've been watching you ever since you got to Seattle. Did you think changing your name would be enough? That requesting a new Social Security number would keep you safe? I own you."

Where was Logan? Why had Brian come in? What was I going to do?

CHAPTER TWENTY-ONE

Logan...

I came to in the hospital, no memory of what had happened. I'd just finished having the best blow job of my life, ensuring I returned the favor to Kaia, when the knock came. It was the clothes she'd ordered so we could go out and get some pizza. I should have looked, but I didn't even think about it.

"Hello," a nurse said as he walked into the room.

"What the fuck happened?" I asked, my voice harsher than it likely needed to be.

"I can tell you what I know," he said, checking my vitals as he talked with me. "But our information is pretty limited. What do you remember?"

"Opening a hotel room door," I said. "After that, everything's blank."

"Do you remember the hotel?"

"Yeah," I said, giving him the name. "Where's Kaia?" I asked because that was the bigger question.

"You came in by yourself," he said. "Aid car was called because some delivery kid walked in on you lying on the floor."

"What day is it?"

"Monday," he said. "Why?"

"Fuck," I muttered. "That was on Saturday. You're saying I've been out for two... three days?"

"Afraid so," he replied. "We're just glad your vitals have stayed solid. Probably has to do with your physique. The rest of the nurses were kinda ogling you and searched your name. How did someone get the jump on you?"

"Trying to figure that out myself," I said. "Was my phone brought in with me? Or anything else?"

"Your phone, yes, and the clothes that were delivered, as well as the ones that were in the suite with you," he explained. "It looked like you'd had company if you know what I mean, but other than a handful of used condoms, there wasn't anything else. You did still have your wallet, with cash in it, though, so at least there's that."

"Fuck," I growled again. "Can I get my phone? I need to call my coach."

"Sure thing," he said, walking over to a little closet thing that was in the room. He pulled the phone out of a bag and brought it over. "If you need a charger, let me know," he said. "I don't know if it was turned off or if it's just died."

I pressed the button on the side to turn it on, but nothing happened.

"Can I get that charger?" I asked, and he nodded, walking out the door and letting it shut behind him.

CHAPTER TWENTY-TWO

Kaia...

It had been five fucking years, and I was right back where I started from. The only difference was that I knew a few things that Brian didn't realize I'd discovered. He wasn't as powerful as I'd believed, and his comment about having watched me the whole time was a lie. There was no way he'd have waited this long if he'd known. It was that fucking party that screwed me up. But that same party gave me something I hadn't had all those years ago – a hope for a better future.

CHAPTER TWENTY-THREE

L ogan...
"Slow down," Coach Wheeler said. "You're not making any sense."

"I need to talk to one of the owners," I said again. "The one who owns the company that came for the event on Friday. It's about one of his employees. She's in danger."

"I have no idea who that is," he said, his voice sounding tired.

"Just get me the name of the company," I said. "I can go from there."

"You know you need to be at the practice facility tomorrow, right?" he asked.

"Saving Kaia's life is more important," I said, and that must have gotten to him.

"I'll figure it out," he said. "Where are you?"

"I'll explain everything as soon as I can," I said. "I'm just getting out of the hospital, but I need to get this done. The longer I wait, the less time she has."

"Let me find that info and I'll call you back," he said.

"Can you text me?" I asked. "I might not be able to answer a call."

"Sure," he said, then disconnected the call.

"Ready?" the nurse asked when he walked into the room.

I'd been given a clean bill of health after a full battery of tests, and I was so ready to get out it was killing me having to wait.

"More than," I replied, getting up off the edge of the bed.

"Hospital policy," he said, indicating the wheelchair.

"Not my first rodeo," I replied, sitting down. "Uber should be at the entrance when we get there."

"Good," he said. "You got someone who can watch you?"

"Team's got a crew," I said. "They'll make sure I'm right as rain."

We headed out of the room, and all the nurses at the station were watching. Some of the family and friends of other patients were also hovering around in the hallway. I didn't need a fucking audience watching me leave, so I put my sunglasses on and ducked my head. The elevator came, and when someone else went to get in with us, the nurse stopped them, saying they could wait. I was thankful for his help on that front. The last thing I wanted to do was get an interrogation from some rando in an elevator.

"Here you go," he said as we went out the front door. "Looks like the timing was perfect."

"Mr. Knox?" a man asked.

"That's me," I said, standing up out of the chair.

"I don't have handicap capabilities," he said. "Your request didn't indicate the need..."

"Hospital has to take me to the curb in that thing," I said. "I'm good to go. No worries."

He'd opened the back door, so I slid in, setting the plastic bag with the rest of the clothes on the seat next to me as he closed it. When he got in, he shut the door, put the car in drive, and pulled away from the entrance to the hospital.

"Do you have a music preference?" he asked.

"Whatever you want is fine," I said.

A classical piece came through the speakers, low in volume, and he drove on, following the directions on his phone. When we pulled up to the practice facility, he put the car in park and went to get out.

"This is good," I said. "Have a good day."

"Thank you," he replied with a nod.

Walking into the building, I followed the signs to the offices, and when I walked in, the owner I'd wanted to talk to was there.

"You're Logan Knox," he said, not a question, but not really a statement, either. "Coach Wheeler said you knew something about one of my employees. Who is it?"

"Can we sit in an office?" I asked. "This is more than a little complicated, and privacy is imperative."

CHAPTER TWENTY-FOUR

K aia...
I'd get out of this, just as I had before, and this time, fuck him if he thought I wouldn't put everything out in public for the world to know who and what he was. He could try to use the contract, the video, all the other shit he said he had against me, but I had the truth. A forty-year-old man should not be grooming a child, then taking advantage of that grooming to force her into a contract she had no clue how to even try to understand. My parents sold me out, and I'd kicked them to the curb. I'd do the same with Brian, because, honestly, I was done.

It was something I should have done when I first left, but I wasn't strong enough then. I am, now, and he will never see it coming. I have faith that Logan will find me, that he will help me, and that he will stand beside me when all the dust settles.

CHAPTER TWENTY-FIVE

L ogan...

"You're absolutely sure?" Mr. Roberts asked me.

I'd told Kaia's story, or at least the parts she'd told me. I explained what happened and why I was in the hospital, and she was in the wind. There was no way I could guarantee she didn't take me for a ride, but what I saw was as real and raw as I'd ever seen.

"If she was lying," I said, remembering the conversation I'd had with Kaia. "Well, she deserves an Oscar for her performance."

"Okay," he said. "I think I can get some answers, but I want to keep you out of it as much as possible."

"He knows I was with her," I said. "Whoever it was that came to get her saw me because I opened the door. I'm surprised he hasn't contacted you to ask you to get rid of me."

"He knows next to nothing about hockey," he said. "In order to get rid of you, he'd have to come up with something pretty convincing, and I just don't see him doing that."

"Did you know?" I asked, and when he looked at me

confused, I elaborated. "Did you know he was this kind of monster?"

"No," he said, and I believed him. "If I did, I'd have never been in any kind of business with him."

"Can you keep her safe?" I asked. "I mean, can you get her away from him? I don't care if she never sees me again. I just don't want her to be left with him."

"Let me see if I can figure out where he is," he said. "Maybe see if he will say something about her."

"I'll let you..."

"Stay," he said, his hand on my arm as I was making to get up and leave. "You've come this far. You deserve some answers."

I sat down, and he set his laptop up on the table in the office. Where I was sitting, he wouldn't see me, so I could listen to the call without him knowing I was there. Instead of watching Mr. Roberts, I closed my eyes.

"Hey," I heard Brian say from the speaker of the laptop.

"Hey, yourself," Mr. Roberts said, no trace of unease in his voice. "I got a strange call today about one of my employees, and they mentioned one of the other owners was connected. I figured, since we've known each other for half our life, I'd start with you. I'm sure it's nothing but just covering my bases."

"Strange, how?" he asked, and I could hear an edge to his voice.

"This guy said he saw you throw a girl in a trunk," he said, elaborating on the non-story I had told him. "I mean, who does that? It's probably a prank or something, but the girl never showed up for work, so I had to check."

"I don't think I've thrown anyone in a trunk since we were in college," the asshole said with a laugh. "Do you remember those sorority sisters we snatched? God, that was forever ago. Good times that was. But no, I haven't thrown anyone into a trunk this week."

"I figured," he said. "By the way, where are you staying while you're out here? Figured I'd swing by and grab a drink with you later if you're up for it."

"I'm at the house out in Roy," Brian said. "I can't remember if you've been here. Let me send you the address. You can come by for dinner and drinks. I'll find some entertainment for us, too. Just like the good old days."

"Sounds good," he said.

"See you later," the asshole said, and then Mr. Roberts closed the laptop.

"I'll check it out," he said to me. "He may not even know that I know what he's doing, so he may slip up."

"I'm coming with you," I said.

"Not gonna happen," he replied. "I know you want to help, and I respect that. More than you know. But trust me, it wouldn't be safe for you, me, or her, if you came with. This will end tonight, though."

Looking at him, I weighed my options, which were fuck all at this point.

"Will you at least tell me when you get her?" I asked.

"I'll bring her to you," he said. "Unless she needs care, in which case, I'll let you know what hospital she's at."

I nodded, accepting that my trust had to be in this guy I didn't know. It killed me, but I had to give up that piece of control.

CHAPTER TWENTY-SIX

K aia...

"Well, little lady," Brian said when he came into the room he had me in. "Tonight, you're gonna show your boss just who you are."

I glared, which was all I could do.

"Oh, that fire's there," he said with a sick smile. "Garrett always liked a challenge. I'm sure he'll enjoy making you work for your keep. Minx will be in to get you ready. She loves to help me in any way she can because she's a good girl."

Fan-fucking-tastic. That sadistic bitch had been my nightmare before, and I'm sure she was punished for my escape, which meant she'd be using all the anger she'd built up against me. All I could do was hope and pray that Brian had been telling the truth when he said my boss, because if Mr. Roberts was coming here, he could be my ticket out. Unless he was in on it all along. If that was the case, I was well and truly fucked.

CHAPTER TWENTY-SEVEN

L ogan...
"Hello?" I answered my phone.
"I've got her," he said. "She's with me, and I'm bringing her to you."

The call dropped as soon as he'd finished, and I looked at it. There was no number that showed up, even though I had the owner's saved in my phone. He'd said he was bringing her to me, which made me believe she wasn't hurt. God, I hoped that was true. Fuck, I hoped everything the owner had said was true.

I OPENED the door to my apartment, and there she was. A little bit haggard, but still beautiful. I didn't even think, just pulled her into my arms and held her. She let out a sob, then sort of crumbled. I went down with her, pulling her onto my lap on the ground because I never thought I'd see her again. Who would have thought that twenty-four hours could create such a connection?

"Come on," Mr. Roberts said after a minute. "Let's get inside."

He helped me help her to her feet, and we went into the living room. I sat on the sofa, and she basically sat on my lap. Mr. Roberts sat on the chair that was across the table from me. To say he looked haunted would be an understatement.

"I'm sorry," she said after a while.

"You did nothing wrong," I replied, kissing the top of her head.

She'd finally stopped shaking, at least, but she was still clinging to me.

"Let me order some food," the owner said. "Anything you want."

"What do you wanna eat?" I asked her, trying to look in her face. She shook her head but wouldn't look at me, which pissed me off. Not at her, of fucking course, but at the asshole who had hurt her. "You want that pizza we talked about? I think that would be good."

Again, she shook her head, her breath hot on my neck as she held on for dear life.

"I'll get some," Mr. Roberts said, getting up and heading out.

When he was gone, I tried again, pressing her away from me just a bit.

"Come on, baby," I pleaded. "I know it was bad, but you're safe now. No one will hurt you again. I promise. Hell, you don't even have to stay with me. I'll buy you a fortress anywhere you want. You get the only key, and you can stay safe from the whole fucking world."

"I don't want you to leave me," she whispered. "Please," she said a little louder, tilting her head. "Please don't ever leave me."

It fucking cut me to the core hearing the absolute terror in her voice. I swore to myself in that moment that I'd fucking kill the man who did this to her.

"I'll do whatever you want," I said. "You're in charge. What you say goes."

The sigh she let out made my resolve even stronger.

CHAPTER TWENTY-EIGHT

EIGHTEEN MONTHS LATER...

K aia...

"Come on, woman," I said, waiting at the door.

"You are the bossiest woman I know," Carmen replied.

"I don't want to be late," I said, tapping my foot.

"Okay, okay," she said as she came out of her room. "Is this okay to wear?"

"I swear," I said, fists on my hips. "You try to change one more time, and I'm leaving you here."

"You're so bossy," she said, but she grabbed her jacket.

She locked the door to her apartment, then we headed down the stairs and out the door. It was still cold and icky, but that was March in Seattle. We weren't too far from the arena, and the number of times we'd made the walk meant that it was easy for us to get there with enough time to get in and settled before the game started.

Even though I never went back to work at Panacea, she and I had kept our friendship. She'd taken me to counseling sessions, doctor appointments, to and from the courthouse, and anywhere else I needed to go. Bringing her with me to every game, paying for her apartment, and anything else, was small change compared to what she'd given me when I needed it most.

Logan had been nothing short of amazing. He never pushed, never argued, never even tried anything. Hell, I felt like I was the pervert when I pushed for sex. But we'd finally found a groove that worked for us. Therapy had been difficult at first, talking about everything, and I mean *everything* I'd dealt with in my life.

When some shit started coming to me in nightmares, I was afraid I'd never feel normal again. Dr. Hargrove was more than qualified to help me through all the trauma, though. She diagnosed me with C-PTSD, which took me a while to understand. Repressed memories are a bitch, that's for sure, and I was glad they found their way back out of my head.

Mr. Roberts, or rather Garrett, as he'd told me to call him, helped me immensely, too. I didn't ever ask him how he found me, how he knew what was going on, or why he took my side against his friend. None of that mattered, though. He was more than just a nice guy. He was a hero as far as I was concerned. He'd hired an attorney to represent me during the criminal portion of the trials that I had to go through, then to get me the biggest fucking settlement anyone in their right mind would be impressed with.

After that, he gave me the option to take over Brian's portion of ownership in the team, and I jumped at it. I had no fucking clue what I was doing with it, but the fact that he'd just let it go like that was more than I could have asked for.

I just bought a house on a small piece of land outside the city. It wasn't fancy by any stretch of the imagination, but it was mine. Paid off, completely in my name, and I could do whatever I wanted with it. Logan and I were going to move in after the season was finished, but we'd already christened damn near every room in it, not that I was complaining.

"Hello, ma'am," Reggie said as we stepped to the entrance. "You are looking just as beautiful as ever, if I do say so myself."

"You're not looking too bad, yourself," I replied.

"And Miss Carmen," he said. "You better watch yourself now. Looking like that just might find you a husband."

"Now, Reggie," she said, her smile bright. "You know I'm waiting for you to ask."

It was the same thing every game. Neither of them were really interested in the other, but they had a nice friendship that extended outside the stadium. I really had found a gem in her and was glad she stuck around.

"You go on, now," he said as we walked past him toward our seats.

There was a box for the owners, but I rarely sat there. I took seats just beyond the bench. That way I was close enough to see Logan, but also near the exit if a panic attack hit me. I didn't flaunt who I was, just wore my *Knox* jersey to support my man. Since my ownership in the team was silent, no pictures were around, so as far as anyone knew, I just had season tickets for the seats. Hell, not even the players knew who I was, other than my connection to Logan.

"Think they'll do the kiss cam again?" Carmen asked as we settled ourselves.

"Don't they always?" I asked back.

"Maybe they'll show us," she said.

"I hope not," I replied. "Last thing I want is someone trying to kiss me. Except you."

She'd told me after a few months that the reason she was all up in my business that night at the party was that she had a sort of crush on me and didn't want me to hook up with someone else. The fact that she was so protective of me just melted my heart, and if I were into women at all, she would be a nice catch. Now, though, she said she didn't see me that way anymore. Not because of everything I'd been through but because she could really see how much I cared about Logan. She knew she'd never stand a chance, even if I were interested in women, so she opted to be my friend instead, and I couldn't have been happier.

The game started, and we were engrossed in the action, watching the men fly up and down the ice, slam into each other, and use their amazing talent to try to score goals. Halfway through the first period, just as the they were coming out of the commercial break, some guy tapped me on the shoulder. I turned to look at him when there was a crash on the glass in front of me. I'd never seen a guy jump that much, but then I turned and saw Logan glaring.

"You see that jersey?" he shouted, pointing at me. The guy looked and nodded. "Yeah, that's my number. She belongs to me. Get your fucking mitts off her. Now."

He shouted the last word and the guy turned and ran up the steps. I looked back at the ice, at Logan, and he was watching him go. When he turned to look at me, he gave me the goofiest grin, pressed his glove to the glass, and gave me a wink. I reached out, pressing my hand to the other side of the glass, and it was as if his calm came through that shield between us, calming me when I hadn't even realized I'd been rattled.

At that moment, I knew I wanted to spend the rest of my life with him.

"Marry me," I said, and he looked at me, confused. I hadn't said it very loud, so I figured he just didn't hear me. I stood up against the glass, put both hands on it, and shouted it again. "Marry me."

"Right now?" he asked.

"Yeah," I said. "Right now."

He laughed, looked at Carmen, who was sitting there and filming the whole thing, then looked back at me.

"Can I finish the game first?"

"Of course," I said.

"Thanks," he replied, pounded the glass twice with his fist, then skated back out onto the ice.

As soon as the game was over, he came and got me, helping me out onto the ice. Kenny Shields, one of the other players, brought out the carpet they use for the National Anthem singer, so at least I didn't have to try to figure out my footing.

When I was finally standing even with him, he kneeled in front of me and pulled out a fucking ring. It had a sapphire centerpiece with ruby chips set around the center stone, all wrapped in platinum, and was the most beautiful thing I'd ever seen in my whole life.

"I've been waiting," he said. "From the first time I saw you, I knew I wanted to spend forever with you. I lost you once, and I swore I wouldn't let it happen again."

I was crying, and I didn't care. The only people in the world at that moment were Logan and me, and he was there, his beautiful face looking at me like I'd hung the moon and created the sport he loved.

"Please tell me you weren't joking," he added, and I saw how nervous he was.

"I wasn't," I said, my voice barely above a whisper.

His smile lit up the entire arena as he slid the ring on my finger. It was then that I heard the roar of the crowd and realized that our intimate moment was played out in front of almost twenty thousand people still in their seats. He got up, pulled me to him, and kissed me senseless.

This was what I'd always dreamed of. Just a man who wanted me for me, not what I could give him. Someone who cherished my soul the way Logan did.

NOTE FROM AUTHOR

Images and Blurbs available upon request.
I would ask that you obtain high quality headshots and cover art images directly through me, rather than taking them from either my website or Amazon, however, blurbs are readily available through both places.

ABOUT THE AUTHOR

Born and raised in the Pacific Northwest, CM Kane was fed a steady diet of sports, particularly baseball. Having this love of the game instilled in her at an early age, she found that nothing was better than getting lost in the game. Storytelling was another gift that was encouraged in her youth, and she's taking to the written word to explore a new aspect to the game she loves.

Social Media and Website Links:

Website:
https://www.authorcmkane.com

Facebook:
https://www.facebook.com/AuthorCMKane

Instagram:
https://www.instagram.com/authorcmkane/

Amazon:
https://www.amazon.com/author/cmkane

BlueSky:
https://bsky.app/profile/authorcmkane.bsky.social

ALSO BY C.M. KANE

Seattle Cascades

1. Extra Innings

2. Caught Stealing

3. Backstop

4. Power Hitter

5. Double Play

5.5. Find a Gap

6. Sweet Spot (Coming Soon)

7. 7th Inning Stretch (Coming Soon)

New Orleans Magicians

1. Choke Up

2. Caught in a Pickle

3. Brand New Ballgame (Coming Soon)

4. Fan Interference (Coming Soon)

5. Flashing the Leather (Coming Soon)

Austin Aces Hockey Club (Shared World)

Power Play

Anthologies

Unnerving: Eclipse

Street Justice (Limited Time)

Fooling Around (Coming April 1, 2025)

Neon Lights & Country Nights (Coming June 1, 2025)

Stand Alone Titles

A Switch in Time